ArtScroll Youth Series®

מסורה

Rabbi Nosson Scherman / Rabbi Meir Zlotowitz
General Editors

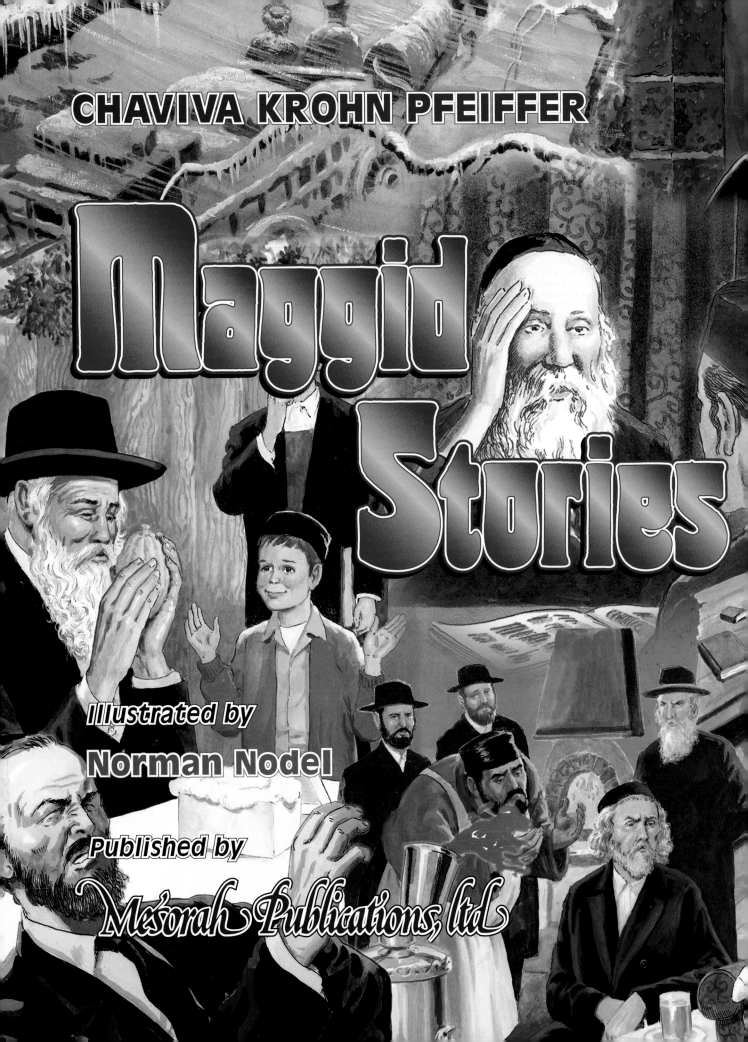

CHAVIVA KROHN PFEIFFER

Maggid Stories

Illustrated by

Norman Nodel

Published by

Mesorah Publications, ltd

for Children

ARTSCROLL YOUTH SERIES®

MAGGID STORIES FOR CHILDREN

© Copyright 1998 by Mesorah Publications, Ltd.
First edition – First impression: November, 1998
        Second impression: July, 1999
        Third impression: November, 2001
        Fourth impression: February, 2006

Published by MESORAH PUBLICATIONS, LTD.
4401 Second Avenue / Brooklyn, N.Y 11232 / (718) 921-9000 / Fax: (718) 680-1875
e-mail: artscroll@mesorah.com

Distributed in Israel by SIFRIATI / A. GITLER
6 Hayarkon Street / Bnei Brak 51127

Distributed in Europe by J. LEHMANN HEBREW BOOKSELLERS
Unit E, Viking Industrial Park, Rolling Mill Road / Jarrow, Tyne and Wear / England NE32 3DP

Distributed in Australia and New Zealand by GOLD'S BOOK & GIFT SHOP
3-13 William Street / Balaclava, Melbourne 3183, Victoria, Australia

Distributed in South Africa by KOLLEL BOOKSHOP
Shop 8A Norwood Hypermarket / Norwood 2196 / Johannesburg, South Africa

Printed in the Israel by Alon Print / +972-2-5388938

ISBN: 1-57819-295-1

TABLE OF CONTENTS

Author's Preface   6

1. A Little Boy's Esrog   8

2. The Hole Truth   12

3. Royal Rescue   14

4. A Dance for the Ages   18

5. Meir'ka   20

6. Brotherly Love   22

7. The Baker's Bread   24

8. House Guests   26

9. A Time to Wait   30

10. A Way to Return   32

11. From Moshe to Moshe   34

12. Garments of Glitter   36

13. Salty Conversation   38

14. The Right Place   40

15. Two Baked Apples   42

16. Memories   44

17. Acts of Kindness   46

AUTHOR'S PREFACE

I am grateful to the *Ribono Shel Olam* for having given me the opportunity to write this collection of stories about *gedolim* and lay people which teach us lessons in *mitzvos, middos* and *hashkafah*.

Stories have always been a focal point in the lives of my siblings and myself. As children, we looked forward to the nights when our father, Rabbi Paysach Krohn, would come into our room and tell us a bedtime story that he made up as he told it, always ending with a lesson from which we could learn. As we grew, our father told us stories of a different nature — stories he had heard as a young man from the renowned Maggid of Jerusalem, Rabbi Sholom Schwadron, *zt"l*. These stories and parables, and many others our father heard around the world, materialized into his four "Maggid" books. Like the stories from our childhood, each brought forth a lesson in a clear and gentle way, to which everyone could relate.

One by one, people in cities and countries the world over discovered what we had known all along: that our father possesses a treasure house of stories, and has been blessed with a uniquely clear and charismatic way of telling them. Thus, the Maggid stories have become known far and wide.

My husband, R' Shlomo Dovid, and I, both being teachers, saw that the powerful message of the Maggid could often be simplified enough to inspire even the very young. And so the idea to transmit these stories to children was born. The stories in this book have been carefully chosen from the four Maggid books that have been published to date. Each teaches a lesson understandable to youngsters, in an uncomplicated plot.

It is my hope that children of all ages will be inspired by these stories, so that they, too, may grow with the Maggid.

I would like to express my deep *hakaras hatov* to my husband, R' Shlomo Dovid, for his constant encouragement and support throughout the writing of this book. As a Rebbe in Yeshiva Toras Chaim of South Shore, he has used these and other stories to impart lessons of *yiras shamayim*, and a love of Torah and *mitzvos.* His popular publication of *Weekly Gems* for the benefit of his *talmidim* was the prototype for this book.

I would also like to thank my children for being the ideal sounding board, as they listened with rapt attention to each story before it was submitted.

I am grateful to Rabbi Nosson Scherman for editing this book. Rabbi Scherman further simplified and clarified each story, breaking down paragraphs and sentences into the most easily understandable text for young children. I am in awe of his talents.

I would also like to thank the entire ArtScroll staff for their work in connection with this book. I am especially grateful to Reb Avrohom Biderman, who smoothly blended the raw materials to make the finished product. I also thank Mr. Norman Nodel, whose beautiful illustrations are key in making the lessons of the Maggid come alive to children.

Most of all, I am grateful to my parents, Rabbi and Mrs. Paysach and Miriam Krohn. They regard each of their children as individuals, and have always encouraged us and expected us to strive to reach our own potential. With this mind-set, we have each, at different stages of our lives, reached deep within ourselves to find the strength to rise to even greater heights, to reach milestones that we may otherwise not have attempted. "כַּבֵּד אֶת ה' מֵהוֹנֶךָ" (משלי ג:ט), we try to make our parents proud by using our capabilities to glorify the Name of Hashem. May Hashem give them the strength to continue their *avodas hakodesh,* inspiring their family and *klal Yisroel.*

I dedicate this book to my grandmother, Mrs. Hindy Krohn, who brought the appreciation and beauty of the written word into the Krohn family. With unbending *emunah* and a strength of character passed down to her by her own parents, she was *zochah* to witness generations of her immediate and extended family grow up as *shomrei Torah u'mitzvos.* (See her book, *The Way It Was,* published by ArtScroll.) May Hashem give her strength to continue to be the role model, confidante, and author we all look up to.

Kew Gardens, New York   Chaviva Pfeiffer
ר"ח כסלו, תשנ"ט

A LITTLE BOY'S ESROG

In Jerusalem, many years ago, Reb Zalman was known to be a great *esrog* expert. Before Succos, hundreds of people would come to his home to ask him if their *esrog* or *lulav* was kosher and beautiful.

One year, Reb Zalman was busy seeing people's *esrogim* until late in the afternoon before Succos.

Finally, the last person left. Reb Zalman quickly prepared his *Yom Tov* clothing and left his house to go to the *mikveh.* On his way, a little boy named Aharon came to him, holding a small white box.

"Reb Zalman," the young boy called out, "could you please check my *esrog*? My father bought it for me."

This boy's father, Rabbi Avrohom Moshe Katzenellenbogen, was a well-known *talmid chacham.* "My child," Reb Zalman said, "if your father bought you the *esrog,* it is surely kosher." And with that he rushed on to the *mikveh.*

Aharon felt bad. He wanted to be like all the grownups. It was his first *esrog,* and he wanted Reb Zalman to tell him how beautiful it was. But Reb Zalman had no time for him. Couldn't he take the time to look at just one more *esrog*? Aharon went home feeling very sad, but he did not tell anyone what had happened.

Early the next morning, the first day of Succos, Aharon was still fast asleep. Reb Avrohom Moshe was learning in his *succah*. There was a knock on the *succah* door. Reb Avrohom Moshe wondered who it could be so early in the morning. He was very surprised when he saw that it was none other than the great Reb Zalman!

"*Gut Yom Tov*!" Reb Avrohom Moshe exclaimed. "What brings you here so early in the morning?"

"I came to see your son Aharon," Reb Zalman answered with a smile. "Is he up yet?"

Reb Avrohom Moshe was surprised. He ran to his son's room. "Aharon, Aharon, wake up! You have a special visitor."

Aharon slowly opened his eyes. "Who is it?" he asked.

"It is Reb Zalman!" his father answered excitedly.

Aharon jumped out of bed, washed *negel vasser,* and got dressed faster than he ever had in his whole life. He hurried to greet his visitor.

"*Gut Yom Tov,* Aharon," Reb Zalman began. "I came to look at your *esrog.*"

"But you told me yesterday that the *esrog* was fine," Aharon said.

"Yes," said Reb Zalman. "I know I told you that, but yesterday I was in a big hurry. I would like to see your *esrog* before you use it for the first time."

Reb Avrohom Moshe watched all this in silence. He began to understand what had happened on *erev Yom Tov.*

Aharon was thrilled. He ran to get his *esrog.* He watched as Reb Zalman checked the *esrog.* He turned it round and round gently, to be sure he did not miss a single spot.

"My dear Aharon," Reb Zalman finally said, "this *esrog* is absolutely beautiful. It is so special that I would even give you my own *esrog* if you would let me have this one."

Aharon smiled. "No, thank you," he said. "I want to use this one because my father picked it for me. But I am very happy that you checked it for me first. Thank you so much!"

Aharon left the *succah* full of joy and pride, holding his precious *esrog* in his hands. He would always remember this Succos.

Reb Avrohom Moshe was amazed at how Reb Zalman had gone out of his way to make Aharon feel special!

As Reb Zalman turned to leave, he said to Reb Avrohom Moshe, "A child is also a person."

We can learn from Reb Zalman always to think of other people's feelings. We should look for ways to make other people happy by saying nice things to them, doing them a favor, greeting them with a smile, or letting them know that they are important.

THE HOLE TRUTH

Most people in Eretz Yisroel use buses to get from place to place. Many of them buy a *cartisia* (bus ticket). Every time they ride a bus, the bus driver punches a hole in the *cartisia*. When the card is used up, they buy a new one.

One afternoon, the Number 3 bus was driving through Jerusalem. At one stop, the driver saw that there were many people waiting to get on. He opened both the front and back doors of the bus and called out, "Tell everyone to get on wherever they find room! Those who get on in the back should pass up their money or *cartisia*."

An eight-year-old boy named Yehudah got in through the back door. He slowly edged up to the driver and held out his *cartisia*.

"I already punched your card," said the driver.

"No, you did not," Yehudah answered softly.

It was a hot day and the driver did not feel like arguing. "Get inside!" he said. "You are blocking the people behind you."

Yehudah looked up at the driver and said in a small voice, "*Ani lo yachol. Zeh geneivah.* (I can't. It is stealing.)"

"I told you, I punched your card," the driver said again. "Get inside."

Yehudah walked down the aisle of the bus. He was very upset. How could he ride the bus if he had not paid?

The bus driver began to drive. Later, he saw in his mirror that Yehudah was crying in the back of the bus.

The driver called him up to the front. "What's the matter, young man? Why are you crying?"

Yehudah held out his *cartisia* again. He said, "*Ani lo yachol. Zeh geneivah.* (I can't. It is stealing.)"

The driver took the *cartisia* from Yehudah's hand, punched a hole in it, and gave it back. Then he patted him on the head and said, "*Attah yeled tov. Zeh yafeh meod.* (You are a good boy. This is very nice.)"

The Torah teaches us to always be honest and tell the truth. Even if other people will not know the difference, Hashem always does.

ROYAL RESCUE

Many years ago, a man named Rabbi Zalman Grossman lived in Jerusalem.

He loved to do *mitzvos,* especially to honor the Shabbos.

Reb Zalman would tell his children, "When the Shabbos Queen comes, I am like the king. I try to stay awake as long as I can to enjoy Shabbos." Reb Zalman did not go to sleep on Shabbos at all. All Friday night he would stay awake, singing *zemiros* and learning Torah. He would *daven* (pray) with great *kavanah* (concentration) and enjoy the delicious Shabbos meals.

Reb Zalman was very poor. He could not make a living in Jerusalem. He came to America and opened an office on the Lower East Side of Manhattan. He worked hard and sent money to his wife and children in Jerusalem.

Reb Zalman lived in a small room behind his office. It had a table and a chair, a bed, and a refrigerator. It wasn't much, but Reb Zalman was happy with what he had.

One Friday night after shul, Reb Zalman came to his room. He was ready to say *Kiddush.* But when he lifted the cup of wine, he suddenly felt a sharp pain in his side. It hurt so much that he dropped the cup of wine and fell to the floor. Reb Zalman cried for help, but there was no one around to help him. He was in too much pain to get to a telephone to call a doctor.

Reb Zalman had a friend named Reb Nachum. He had also come to America so he could earn money for his family in Jerusalem. After Reb Nachum finished his Shabbos meal, he went for a walk. He walked and walked. He thought about what happened to him that week … He thought about the *parashah* of the week … He thought about his family back in Jerusalem whom he missed very much …

Then Reb Nachum looked around. "Where am I?" he thought. He was lost! Then he saw that he was very close to his friend Reb Zalman's office.

"Reb Zalman never sleeps on Shabbos," thought Reb Nachum. "Even though it is very late, I know he is still awake. I will go to his office and spend the night with him."

Reb Nachum walked to Reb Zalman's office and knocked on the door. No one answered. "That's strange," he thought. "I know Reb Zalman is inside, and I'm sure he is not sleeping." He knocked again. He knocked louder. He called Reb Zalman's name. Still, there was no answer.

Now Reb Nachum was worried. He put his ear to the door and listened. Was that the sound of someone moaning in pain?

Reb Nachum ran outside to try to get help. A police car was just passing by! He waved to the police car to stop. He told the two policemen that his friend seemed to be very sick.

The officers broke the door open and, sure enough, there was Reb Zalman, lying on the floor in pain, unable to move.

The police rushed him to the hospital, where the doctors took care of him at once. Reb Nachum went along to be sure everything would be all right.

After a long time, the doctor told Reb Nachum, "Your friend needed an operation. He will need to stay in the hospital for a few days, but he will be fine." Then the doctor said, "It's a good thing you found him when you did, and not an hour later. You really saved his life!"

But Reb Nachum knew that **he** had not saved Reb Zalman's life. **Hashem** had saved his life, because of the way he kept the Shabbos. As we sing in the Shabbos *zemiros*: כִּי אֶשְׁמְרָה שַׁבָּת קֵל יִשְׁמְרֵנִי, *If I keep Shabbos, Hashem will watch over me.*

Reb Zalman kept Shabbos in a very special way, so Hashem watched over him and brought Reb Nachum to save his life.

A Dance for the Ages

Once a wealthy man came to Jerusalem for a visit. He met Rabbi Yehudah Ackerman, whom everyone called Yidel.

Yidel said that he had to raise a lot of money for the Stoliner Yeshivah. The man said, "Do your best, and tomorrow night I will give you $10,000."

Yidel could not believe it. This man would give him so much money?! "Thank you so much!" he said.

The next night, Yidel went to the man's hotel. The man gave him $10,000 and asked, "Aren't you wondering why I did this?"

"I sure am," answered Yidel. "This is a miracle!"

"Sit down, Yidel. I will tell you a story. Then you will understand.

"When I was young, my family was very poor. My parents could not even afford to buy me a hat to wear to my wedding. I went into a hat store and I said to the owner, 'I am getting married tonight and my parents cannot buy me a hat because we are so poor. Could you please give me a hat? I will pay you tomorrow, with money that I will get tonight as wedding presents.'

"The owner said, 'You look like an honest yeshivah boy. I will give you a hat. Mazel tov!'

"I left the store feeling happy. Then I went into a liquor store. I told the owner, 'I am getting married tonight and my parents cannot buy liquor for the wedding because we are so poor. Could you please give me some liquor? I will pay you tomorrow, with money that I will get tonight as wedding presents.'

"The owner of the liquor store said, 'You look like an honest yeshivah boy. Take some bottles of liquor. You can pay me tomorrow. Mazel tov!'

"I left the liquor store in a very good mood. Then, Yidel, I saw you walking down the street. I knew that you are a wonderful dancer. The way you dance at weddings makes the *chasan* (groom) and *kallah* (bride) so happy. I said to you, 'Rabbi Ackerman, you don't know me, but I am getting married tonight. Would you please come to dance at my wedding?'

"That night, in the middle of the wedding, you ran in! Everyone stopped to watch you. They clapped and sang without stop. You helped to make that night the most special one of my life. I was so grateful! I made up my mind

that some day I would repay you. Tonight, I gave you $10,000 because you were nice to me many years ago, when you didn't even know me."

The next time Rabbi Ackerman came to America, he heard that this man's son was getting married. In the middle of the wedding, Yidel ran in to dance for the *chasan* and *kallah* — and for his friend who had helped him so much in Jerusalem.

Afterwards, the man hugged Yidel and said, "How can I ever thank you? You made me remember the happiest night of my life."

Hashem destroyed the Second *Beis HaMikdash* because Jews did not help each other. They used to fight and argue for no reason. If we try to help each other whenever we can, like the people in this story, we will help bring *Mashiach* closer.

MEIR'KA

ne afternoon, Rabbi Sholom Schwadron was sitting in his house, learning. Suddenly, he heard screaming from outside. His wife rushed in and said, "Our neighbor's son Meir'ka fell! He is bleeding over the eye." Reb Sholom ran outside to help the little boy. His Rebbetzin followed him with a wet towel.

Reb Sholom picked up Meir and pressed the wet towel over the cut. Then he ran up the road to bring Meir to the doctor.

Meir's grandmother was walking down the road. From far away, she saw Reb Sholom running up the road holding a crying child. She thought it was his child. "Don't worry," she called out. "Hashem will help. Everything will be all right." But Reb Sholom kept running.

As he came closer, the lady could see that Reb Sholom was holding a little boy. "That boy is not Reb Sholom's son," the lady thought. "I wonder who he is."

When Reb Sholom came even closer, she saw that the boy was her own grandson! "Meir'ka! *Oy vey*, my Meir'ka!" she cried, as she took the boy from Reb Sholom.

The neighbors called out from their windows, "Don't worry! Hashem will help. Everything will be all right."

As long as the lady thought someone else's child was hurt, she was calm enough to say, "Don't worry." But once she realized that it was her own grandson, things seemed much worse.

When another person's toy breaks, or their feelings are hurt, we are quick to say, "Don't worry. Everything will be all right." But when the same thing happens to us, what do we say then? It seems to bother us much more if our own toys or feelings are involved.

We should be as careful with other people's problems and their belongings as we are with our own.

Meir'ka / 21

BROTHERLY LOVE

Reb Chatzkel was in his office in Manhattan. He was a very busy man. Important papers were piled up on his desk. He had to be on the phone a lot. People came to talk to him.

His secretary called him over the intercom. "Someone very important has come to see you! I think it is your Rebbe."

Reb Chatzkel was shocked. His *Rebbe*?! The Kopitchinitzer Rebbe, Rav Avrohom Yehoshua Heschel, had come to see *him*? What made him come?

Reb Chatzkel ran to the waiting room to greet the Rebbe and bring him into his office. "Why did the Rebbe have to come to me?" he asked. "I would have come to Brooklyn to the Rebbe's home. I feel very bad that the Rebbe took the trouble to come all the way here."

The Rebbe smiled gently and said, "Do not feel bad, Reb Chatzkel. The trip was no bother at all. I came here because I need your help."

"Rebbe, please tell me how I can help you," said Reb Chatzkel.

The Rebbe began speaking slowly. "I know a family that needs *tzedakah* very badly. The father has no job, and the mother cannot work because she has to take care of her children. They hardly have enough money to buy food. Would you please give me some money for this poor family?"

"Of course, of course," Reb Chatzkel said. "I will give you a lot of money. But I do not understand. Is that why the Rebbe had to come to my office? The Rebbe could have called me on the telephone and I would have sent a check right away."

"No, no," answered the Rebbe. "This is very important, so I wanted to come myself."

Reb Chatzkel took out his checkbook and his pen. "To whom should I write the check?"

The Rebbe waited a moment. Then he said, "Make out the check to your brother."

Reb Chatzkel was shocked. His very own brother! Reb Chatzkel gave *tzedakah* to all types of poor people. Yet he never thought about his own brother! Now Reb Chatzkel understood why the Rebbe had come all the way to Manhattan. He wanted to teach Reb Chatzkel that a brother should be the **first** one to be helped, not the last.

Many of us help our friends all the time. We help them with schoolwork, we let them use our favorite toys, or lend them money when they ask us. But sometimes we need to be reminded that it is just as important to do *chesed* (kindness) for our fathers and mothers, and brothers and sisters, as it is to help a friend.

THE BAKER'S BREAD

Nosson owned a bakery in the city of Poltava, Russia. His son-in-law Meir worked in the bakery with him.

After World War I, Russia was a very poor country. Food was hard to get. Every family was allowed to buy only a small amount of bread each day. People had to wait on long lines outside the bakery every morning to buy bread.

One cold winter morning, Nosson noticed a yeshivah student waiting on line. He was shivering. Nosson brought him inside through the back door of the warm bakery. "Who are you?" Nosson asked. "Do you live in Poltava?"

The boy answered, "My friends and I learn in the Mirrer Yeshivah. The yeshivah split up because of the war. We are in Poltava with our *Rosh Yeshivah*, Rabbi Lazer Yudel Finkel."

"I will make sure that the yeshivah has fresh bread every day," said Nosson. "Here, have a glass of hot tea. Wait here while I bake some fresh loaves of bread right now."

When the loaves were baked, Nosson piled them into his wagon. "Come with me," he told the boy. "You can show me the way."

And so, Nosson, Meir, and the boy rode to the shul where the *bachurim* (young men) were learning, and delivered the bread.

Every day, Meir would deliver fresh bread to the Mirrer Yeshivah. And every day, Reb Lazer Yudel and the boys would thank Meir for his kindness. This went on until the *Rosh Yeshivah* and his students were able to leave Russia and go back to Mir.

Many years passed. Nosson died, and Meir wanted to leave Russia to live in Israel. But in those years it was very hard for Jews to leave Russia.

After years of waiting, Meir finally got permission to go to Israel. When he got there, he was already very old. It was hard for him to see, and a doctor told him he would need an operation on his eyes. Meir was afraid to be in a hospital alone in a strange country. He decided to try and find some of his old friends from the Mirrer Yeshivah. Maybe some of them had moved to Israel, like him.

Someone told him that there was a yeshivah called Mir in Jerusalem. He

went there, and met Reb Lazer Yudel's daughter, Rebbetzin Chana Miriam Shmulevitz.

When the Rebbetzin saw Meir, she exclaimed, "Meir the baker! You brought us bread every day in Poltava. If not for you, we would have gone hungry!"

The Rebbetzin and Meir sat and talked about the days when he would come riding in his wagon early in the morning with the fresh loaves of bread. "You were so good to us," she told him. "I wish I could do something for you. Do you need anything? Can I help you with something?"

Meir told the Rebbetzin that he needed an operation on his eyes, but he did not know how to find a good doctor or hospital. He had no family to help him. The Rebbetzin said she would take care of everything. She asked her son-in-law, Rabbi Yitzchok Ezrachi, to take Meir to Shaarei Tzedek Hospital. There, a famous doctor did the operation. While Meir was in the hospital, *bachurim* from the yeshivah came to visit him every day.

After the operation, Meir was able to see again. He would come to visit the Mirrer Yeshivah very often. He knew he would always have friends there who would be good to him, just as he had been good to the Mirrer students in Poltava, so many years before.

HOUSE GUESTS

The snow was falling quickly that night. A cold wind was blowing the snow in all directions. Rabbi Yoshe Ber (Yosef Dov) Soloveitchik, the Rav of Brisk, was traveling home with his wagon driver, Yankel. Yankel could hardly see because of the snow.

Suddenly the two travelers saw the light of an inn down the road. "*Baruch Hashem*!" said Reb Yoshe Ber. "A place to spend the night!" It was already late at night, but they were sure the innkeeper would let them in from the freezing cold.

When they reached the inn, Yankel knocked on the door, but nobody answered. The innkeeper had already gone to sleep and he did not want to leave his warm, comfortable bed to bother with guests. Yankel was a strong man. He pounded on the door with all his might. Finally the innkeeper yelled from the upstairs window, "What do you want so late at night? Can't you see this place is closed?"

"Please let us in," Yankel called back. "We are freezing out here. We cannot travel any further because of the snow."

A few minutes later the innkeeper came downstairs and let the two men inside. "Couldn't you find another place to stay?" he complained. He showed them to a small side room. The room was cold and uncomfortable, but it was much better than being outside in the snow. Reb Yoshe Ber and Yankel went to bed.

A short while later, there were loud noises from outside. "Open up in there!" the voice said. "Rabbi Aharon Koidonover and his *chassidim* are here!" Reb Aharon was a famous chassidic Rebbe. The innkeeper jumped out of bed and looked out his window. There were almost twenty people outside! He rushed to open the door.

"Come in! Come in!" he said happily. "I have room for all of you!" The innkeeper seated them at a large table and served cake and tea. Soon everyone was warm and refreshed.

When the Rebbe left the room to wash his hands, he noticed a man in the small side room. When he took a closer look, he saw that it was the great Brisker Rav! "*Oy vey!* Brisker Rav!" he exclaimed. "Why are you in this cold room? Come with me!" He brought Reb Yoshe Ber and Yankel into the large room with all the *chassidim.*

Reb Aharon turned to his *chassidim* and said, "Do you see who is in this inn with us? The *gadol hador* (leader of the generation), Rabbi Yoshe Ber Soloveitchik!"

Then he turned to the innkeeper and said, "I cannot believe what you did! How could you have put such a great *tzaddik* in that small, cold room? You must ask him to forgive you."

"I am sorry," the innkeeper said softly to Reb Yoshe Ber. "I did not know who you were."

Reb Yoshe Ber looked straight at the innkeeper and said, "I cannot forgive you."

The innkeeper asked for forgiveness again, but the Rabbi did not forgive him.

"The way you treated the Rabbi and his driver was very wrong," Reb Aharon said to the innkeeper. "You must get him to forgive you."

The innkeeper begged and pleaded for forgiveness, but Reb Yoshe Ber did not answer. The *chassidim* could not understand why he did not want to forgive the innkeeper. Finally, Reb Yoshe Ber began to speak in a low voice.

"My dear friend," he said to the innkeeper. "Of course I will forgive you. But first I want you to understand what you did wrong. You think that you should be nice only to people like the Koidonover Rebbe and the Brisker Rav. That is wrong. You must be kind to *everyone,* especially on a cold, snowy night. I hope that you will change your ways. Also, the next time you come to Brisk, I would like you to be my guest."

The innkeeper was happy that the Rav had forgiven him. He promised to be nice to everyone.

A few weeks later, the innkeeper was in Brisk. He stayed at Reb Yoshe Ber's home. The Rav treated the innkeeper with great respect, and gave him everything he needed.

When the innkeeper got back home, he remembered what the Brisker Rav had taught him. From then on, he made sure to greet his guests warmly and be nice to them. Soon his inn became the most popular one around.

Shammai taught: הֱוֵי מְקַבֵּל אֶת כָּל הָאָדָם בְּסֵבֶר פָּנִים יָפוֹת, *Greet every person with a cheerful face (Avos 1:15).* We should greet every person with a

smile, and treat everyone the way we would treat someone who is very famous and important.

A TIME TO WAIT

Rav Yisroel Meir HaKohen Kagan, the Chafetz Chaim, lived in Radin, a small town in Poland.

He had a young relative named Leib, who was learning in a yeshivah. Leib was on a train going home for Shabbos. The train made extra stops along the way, and Leib saw that it was getting late.

"*Oy vey*," he thought to himself. "Today is Friday. I cannot stay on this train. I will not get home in time for Shabbos!"

Leib asked the conductor where the train would stop on the way. He hoped that they would stop at a Jewish town where he could spend Shabbos. He was very happy to hear that they would stop near Radin, where the Chafetz Chaim lived!

The train finally arrived in a town near Radin late on Friday afternoon. Leib took his suitcases and ran to the Chafetz Chaim's house.

When he got there, the Rebbetzin welcomed him kindly. "Come inside," she told Leib. "My husband has already gone to shul. He always learns before Shabbos starts. Put down your things, and rest for a while on the couch. You must be very tired. You can go to shul when Shabbos starts."

Leib was exhausted. The train was not comfortable, so he had hardly slept the night before. He lay down on the couch and was soon fast asleep.

When Leib woke up, it was dark outside. The Chafetz Chaim was sitting at the Shabbos table with a *sefer*.

"*Gut Shabbos*," said the Chafetz Chaim when he noticed that Leib was awake. "Welcome to our home. We are honored to have you as our guest. I hope you have had a good rest. Please, go wash *negel vasser*, *daven Kabbalas Shabbos* and *Maariv*, and then you can join us for the Shabbos meal."

When Leib finished *davening*, the Chafetz Chaim called his wife. He then said *Kiddush*, and the three of them ate the meal together. At the end of the meal, the Chafetz Chaim went to his room to go to sleep.

Leib tried to fall asleep, but he was not tired anymore. After a while, he got up and went to the kitchen. He looked at the clock and could not believe what he saw. He looked again. The clock read 4:00 — it was the middle of the night! Had they finished the *seudah* (meal) so late that it was almost morning? He looked out the window, but it was still dark outside. He could not tell if it was the beginning of the night or the end. Leib was confused, but he went back to the couch. After a while he fell asleep.

When Leib woke up in the morning, he saw the Rebbetzin. "*Gut Shabbos*," he said. "Last night, after the *seudah* ended, I could not fall asleep, so I came into the kitchen. The clock read 4:00. Was that the right time?"

"Yes," the Rebbetzin answered. "We finished the Shabbos meal quite late."

"But I don't understand," said Leib. "The meal did not take long. Did I sleep for a very long time before the meal began?"

The Rebbetzin smiled. "I'll tell you the truth," she said. "When my husband came home from shul, you were in a very deep sleep. He said we should not wake you up because you were so tired from your trip. It was getting late, so my husband told our son Aharon to say *Kiddush*. Aharon and I ate the *seudah* while the Chafetz Chaim learned. He would not start his meal without you. When you woke up, it was already very late. He called me, and we sat with you for the *Shabbos seudah*. That is why the meal ended so late."

Leib was amazed. The great *tzaddik*, the Chafetz Chaim, had waited up especially for him! And besides this, the Chafetz Chaim did not even tell him that he had waited so long for him. He found out only because he noticed the clock, and asked the Rebbetzin what had happened. He never forgot that great lesson in *hachnasas orchim* (taking in guests).

A Way to Return

One Friday morning, Mr. Josh Braunstein was driving to work when he remembered that he had to make an important telephone call. He stopped at a phone booth and went inside.

As he dialed, Josh saw a thick office-planner notebook stuffed with papers and notes, lying on top of the phone. "Someone must have forgotten this here," he thought. "I will take it and do the *mitzvah* of returning something that is lost."

He looked inside the cover for the owner's name, address, and phone number, but he could not find them. In the book there were telephone numbers of people from all over America, including the numbers of some rabbis.

When Josh got to his office, he checked the page in the book for that day, August 19. He was hoping to find the phone numbers of the people the owner might be meeting that day, but it was no use. The book was filled with papers and information, but Josh could not find a clue about its owner.

When he came home that afternoon for Shabbos, he showed the book to his wife. After Shabbos Mrs. Braunstein opened the book. She found a clue. At the end of the book, it said "Mom," with a phone number. "This is the phone number of the owner's mother!" she said. "I'll call her right now."

Mrs. Braunstein called the lady and said, "My husband found an office-planner book in a phonebooth. We are Jewish and it is a *mitzvah* to return a lost object to its owner. I found your number in the book. Do you have a child who may have lost this?"

"It sounds like it might be my daughter's," said the lady.

The lady gave Mrs. Braunstein her daughter's name and phone number. Then the two women continued talking for about half an hour.

On Sunday morning, the young woman who had lost the book came to the Braunsteins' house. "Thank you for trying so hard to find me," she said. "I was looking all over for that book. I am so happy to have it back!"

The next Friday, she brought the Braunsteins a huge bouquet of flowers. She said, "My family does not know much about *Yiddishkeit*. I grew up not knowing about Torah, Shabbos, or eating kosher. About five years ago I began to realize how special it is to do *mitzvos*. I started to learn more and more, and now I am religious. But my mother was not happy. She said, 'What is wrong with the way I do things? Why don't you want to be like me?' For the last five years, we have not spoken to each other as much as we used to.

"When you called my mother, you explained why you were trying to find me — to do a *mitzvah*. She called me and said, 'If that is what religious Jews are like, then I understand why you want to be like them.' All week long she has been telling her friends about you. My mother and I talked to each other many times this week. We became very close, just like we used to be!"

This story teaches us to always look for ways to do *chesed*, so that we will make a *Kiddush Hashem* and bring others closer to *Yiddishkeit*.

FROM MOSHE TO MOSHE

Rabbi Chaim Moshe Yehudah Schneider was the *Rosh Yeshivah* of Yeshivah Toras Emes in London. The Grozhinsky family owned a bakery near the yeshivah. They told Rabbi Schneider that the yeshivah could have all their extra bread and cake. Every day a different student went to pick up the bread from the bakery.

Some of the boys did not like this job. When their turn came, they would say, "I don't want to carry that heavy bag of bread. The crumbs will get all over me, and people will stare at me."

There was one boy named Moshe who never complained when it was his turn. He even went when other boys did not want to.

Rabbi Schneider wanted his students to wake up early in the morning to learn Torah before *davening*. He needed one boy to wake everyone on time. A different boy named Moshe offered to do the job. Moshe woke up every morning at 5:00 a.m. and made sure that everyone was awake in time.

One day, while Rabbi Schneider was teaching, he said, "Moshe Reichmann, who is always happy to pick up the bread for us, will someday be so rich that the entire world will know about his wealth; and Moshe Shternbuch, who gets up so early to make sure that others will learn, will be such a *talmid chacham* that the entire Torah world will know of his wisdom."

Both of these things came true. Moshe Reichmann became a very rich man. He gives *tzedakah* to yeshivos and poor people all over the world.

Rabbi Moshe Shternbuch is a Rav in Eretz Yisrael and South Africa. He has written many well-known *sefarim.*

Hashem rewarded both of these great people for the kind deeds they did when they were young.

GARMENTS OF GLITTER

Reb Asher and his wife Reichel lived in a small town in Poland. They were poor, and their clothing was worn and ragged, but they and their children were happy with what they had.

One winter, Reb Asher decided to save money so he could buy material to make a new dress for his wife and a suit for himself. He wanted both in time for Pesach.

A few weeks before Pesach, Reb Asher had saved enough money. He traveled to the big city of Vilna to buy material for the clothing.

When he got to Vilna, he saw that the people were very excited. The Romm family had just printed the first *Gemaras* of their new *Shas*. They were being sold in stores that very day!

Reb Asher was curious. He went into a store to look at the new *Gemaras*. His eyes lit up when he saw how bright and beautiful they were. "How my son Aharon Leib would love such brand new *Gemaras*!" he thought. He touched the money in his pocket. "No," he told himself. "I cannot spend all my money on these *Gemaras* and disappoint Reichel. She would feel very bad if I told her she will not have a new dress after all."

Then Reb Asher said to himself, "But if I buy these *Gemaras* for Aharon Leib, he will be so excited. He will rush to yeshivah every day to learn from such beautiful *sefarim* (books). What could be more important than my son's Torah learning? Maybe we will have a new suit and dress next year, but now I will buy these *Gemaras* instead. I am sure Reichel will understand."

Reb Asher took all the money that he had worked so hard to save and spent it on the brand-new *Gemaras*.

When he came home, Reb Asher said to Reichel, "Look what I bought in Vilna for Aharon Leib! He loves to learn Torah so much, and now he will be even more excited to learn."

Reichel did not even ask if she could still have a new dress. She just held one of the special *Gemaras* in her hands and said softly, "This is the most beautiful thing I have ever seen. I am so happy you bought it. Come, let us go right now to the yeshivah and give it to Aharon Leib."

When the parents came to the yeshivah, they were crying from happiness.

Aharon Leib stood in amazement as they gave him his new *Gemara*. "Here is my dress," said Reichel. "This is for you, my son. Learn well!"

"Here is my suit," said Reb Asher. "Use it well, my child. Your Torah learning is the most important thing in the world to us."

Aharon Leib used his gift very well. He grew up to become a *talmid chacham* and the Rav of a city. His son, Rabbi Avrohom Kalmanowitz, became the Rabbi of Tiktin, Poland, and the president of the Mirrer Yeshivah in Poland. He later was the *Rosh Yeshivah* of the Mirrer Yeshivah in Brooklyn. Aharon Leib's grandson, Reb Shraga Moshe, was also the *Rosh Yeshivah* of the Mirrer Yeshivah in Brooklyn.

Reb Asher and Reichel showed that Hashem's Torah is worth all the time and money we have.

RABBI AVROHOM KALMANOWITZ

SALTY CONVERSATION

The Chafetz Chaim was always very careful not to speak or listen to *lashon hara.*

Once, he and another rabbi were traveling together. They stopped at an inn to eat lunch. The woman who owned the inn saw that two rabbis had come! She sat them at a special table and served them right away.

When they finished eating lunch, the woman asked them, "How did you like the food?"

The Chafetz Chaim said, "It was delicious. Thank you for serving us."

The other rabbi said, "The food was very good, but it needed a little more salt."

When the woman went back to the kitchen, the Chafetz Chaim said to the other rabbi, "How could you have said such a thing? All my life I have been careful not to speak or hear *lashon hara,* and now you have caused me to listen to *lashon hara!*"

The rabbi was surprised. "Why are you so upset?" he asked. "I told the woman the food was good. I just said that it needed some salt. Is that so bad?"

"You do not understand," answered the Chafetz Chaim. "That woman owns the inn. A different lady cooks the food. When you said that the food needed salt, you were saying that the cook is not good. Now the owner is in the kitchen telling the cook what you said. The cook will say that she really did put in enough salt, and that would be a lie. The owner will scream at the cook and make her feel bad. She may even fire her. Maybe the cook is very poor and needs the money for her family. So many bad things will happen because you said something not nice."

The rabbi looked at the Chafetz Chaim and said softly, "I understand that I said something wrong, but I do not think it is as bad as you say."

"Let us go to the kitchen and see," said the Chafetz Chaim.

The two men went to the kitchen. The owner was yelling at the cook. "Didn't I tell you to use more salt? How can I let you work here if I will be embarrassed by your cooking?" The cook began to cry as she thought about her poor, hungry children.

When the rabbi saw all this, he ran over to the cook and said, "Please forgive me. The food really did taste very good." Then he said to the owner, "Please, let the cook keep her job. The meal was excellent! She is doing a fine job."

The owner smiled and said, "Of course she can keep her job. I just wanted her to be a little more careful."

We can learn from the Chafetz Chaim to think before we speak. Even a little bit of *lashon hara* can do a lot of harm.

THE RIGHT PLACE

Rabbi Yisroel and Faigele Reichner had eight sons and three daughters. The boys had many rebbe'im at *cheder* (school), but their favorite rebbe was Rabbi Lazer Katz. He did not just teach the boys *Gemara*. He taught them to love Torah and *mitzvos*, just as he did.

When Reb Lazer became old, he could not teach anymore. Mrs. Reichner knew that Reb Lazer had very little money. Every afternoon she would send him food for lunch and supper. Before every Yom Tov, she also sent money, so that Reb Lazer could buy something for himself. She did this for more than twenty years!

When Reb Lazer was very old, he died. Rabbi and Mrs. Reichner died also.

❊ ❊ ❊

Many years passed. One of the eight Reichner boys, Ashi, and his wife, Miriam, lived in Pressburg. They had always been very happy in their town. They had lots of Jewish and gentile friends. Life was good.

Then, in the early 1940s things began to change. German enemies of the Jews started to make trouble. Gangs began to hurt Jews and break their windows. It was getting worse and worse. One day Ashi and Miriam heard that a big gang was coming and they were planning to kill Jews.

Ashi and Miriam knew they had to leave their home and hide somewhere — but where should they go?

"I heard there is a place on the *left* side of the city to hide," Ashi told his wife.

"I heard there is a place on the *right* side of the city to hide," Miriam said.

They could not decide which way to run. Finally Ashi said, "*Chazal* tell us that women can feel what is right. Let us run to the right side of the city."

They came to the small apartment of Anna Neni, a kind, old gentile woman who was hiding Jews. They knocked on her door and she let them in. She showed them that behind a closet, she had two secret rooms where twelve Jewish people were already hiding. Ashi and Miriam were especially happy to see that their daughter, son-in-law, and grandchild were there too! Every

day, Anna Neni would go to the store and buy food for the people. The Reichners lived with Anna Neni peacefully for eight months, until it was safe to come out.

Anna Neni's apartment, where the Reichner family was saved, used to be the apartment of Reb Lazer Katz. In the same place where Ashi's mother, Mrs. Faigele Reichner, had helped Reb Lazer by sending him food and money, Hashem protected her children, grandchildren and great-grandchild!

When we do a *chesed,* Hashem always rewards us for it. Hashem may do a *chesed* for us in return. Or He may save the *zechus* (merit) of the *chesed,* and reward us by helping our children and grandchildren.

Two Baked Apples

Reb Yosef is a friendly man who greets everyone with a smile.

One day, he went into a restaurant to eat lunch. As he was walking in, he saw an old, poor man sitting there. "Hello, Reb Berel," he said to the man. "How are you today? Come, have lunch with me. I do not like to eat alone. Let me buy you something to eat."

"No, thank you," said Reb Berel. "I am not in the mood to eat, but I will sit with you."

The two men sat down at a table. "Reb Berel, you must be hungry," said Reb Yosef. "Please, have something to eat."

"All right," Reb Berel answered. "I'll have two baked apples and a glass of tea."

The two men sat together, talking and eating.

Later that day, Reb Yosef was at home, getting ready for a business trip.

"Why do you have to drive tonight?" his wife asked him. "It is supposed to rain and be very windy tonight. It is dangerous to drive in bad weather. Go in the morning."

"Don't worry," Reb Yosef answered. "I know the roads very well. Besides, it is not even raining yet. If the weather gets very bad, I can sleep over in a motel."

As Reb Yosef started his trip, it began to rain lightly. Soon it began to rain harder. Then the wind started to blow and the rain came pouring down. Before he knew it, his car was skidding across the highway. Cars were coming at him from the other direction! Reb Yosef heard a crash and the sound of glass shattering.

At first he did not know where he was. When he came to his senses, he saw that his car was stuck in a ditch on the side of the highway. Reb Yosef tried to get out of his car, but the door was very hard to open. He finally squeezed himself out and climbed out of the ditch.

People who saw what had happened called for help. Two tow trucks came and pulled the car out of the ditch. Reb Yosef went along to the service station in one of the tow trucks. "It is too dangerous to drive tonight. You should spend the night nearby," someone said.

Just then Reb Yosef remembered that his friends, the Friedmans, had a small hotel not far away. He called them and they said they would wait up until he came. The tow company called a taxi for him.

It was after midnight when Reb Yosef got to the hotel.

"Come inside," said Mr. Friedman. "It is so good to see you. *Baruch Hashem* you are not hurt."

"You must be very tired," said Mrs. Friedman. "Sit down and have something to eat. I just made these."

And she put before Reb Yosef two baked apples and a glass of tea.

Reb Yosef could hardly believe his eyes. Two baked apples and a glass of tea? Wasn't that exactly what he had bought for Reb Berel earlier in the day?

Reb Yosef is sure that Hashem was showing him that his life had been saved because of the *tzedakah* he had given Reb Berel.

MEMORIES

When Rabbi Pinchos Hirschprung was a young man, he was one of the best students in the yeshivah of Rabbi Meir Shapiro, in Lublin.

Once, Rabbi Shapiro needed to send someone to America to collect money for the yeshivah. He asked Reb Pinchos to go.

Reb Pinchos thought it would be a good idea to ask the *gadol hador,* Rabbi Chaim Ozer Grodzinsky, to write a letter about the great Yeshivah Chachmei Lublin. When the people in America would read the letter, they would see how important it was to give money to help the yeshivah.

Reb Pinchos traveled to a little town near Vilna to visit Reb Chaim Ozer. Even though Reb Chaim Ozer was old and weak, he took the time to write a letter for the yeshivah. He read the letter over to himself and said, "This letter is not good enough." He wrote a new letter, to be sure that the people in America would understand how important it was to give *tzedakah* for the great yeshivah in Lublin.

After he wrote the letter, Reb Chaim Ozer began to talk to Reb Pinchos about what he was learning in yeshivah. The other people in the room listened in amazement. Both the great *tzaddik* and the young *talmid* knew so much about so many areas of the Torah!

Then Reb Chaim Ozer quoted something and said, "It is in the *Gemara Yoma,* on *daf mem tes* (page 49)."

Reb Pinchos thought those words were on a different page. "Excuse me, Rebbe, but I think those words are on *daf mem ches* (page 48)," the young man said.

"No," said Reb Chaim Ozer, "they are on *daf mem tes.*"

"I'm sure I'm right," thought Reb Pinchos. "But how can I correct the great *gaon* again? That would not be *derech eretz* (respect)." Instead he said, "Maybe there is a *Gemara* here and we can look it up."

"It's all right," Reb Chaim Ozer answered. "Let's not check. You are young and your mind is clear. You are probably right. I am already old. Maybe I forgot exactly where the words are. If we look it up I might be embarrassed."

Reb Pinchos felt bad for Reb Chaim Ozer. He surely did not want to embar-

rass him. He did not get a *Gemara* to check who was right.

After talking to Reb Chaim Ozer a little more, Reb Pinchos thanked him for the letter and left.

A little while later, Reb Pinchos decided to look up the *Gemara* to see who was right. He was shocked! The words were on *daf mem tes*! Reb Chaim Ozer had been right and he had been wrong.

"Now I understand why Reb Chaim Ozer did not want me to look up the *Gemara* while I was in his house," thought Reb Pinchos. "He knew that if I would look up the *Gemara,* and see that I was wrong, I would be embarrassed in front of all the people in the room. He made believe *he* was wrong, just so that I would not be embarrassed."

ACTS OF KINDNESS

R abbi Avrohom Zelig Krohn was a wise, kind man. He loved to learn Torah and teach it to his children. He and his wife, Mrs. Hindy Krohn, always looked for ways to help other people. They especially loved to do the *mitzvah* of *hachnasas orchim.* All types of people were welcome in the Krohn home. All the guests remembered their special stay long after they had left the Krohns.

Once, a young man from Eretz Yisroel named Rafi was the Krohns' Shabbos guest. He told the Krohns about many different people in Eretz Yisrael. One of these people was Rabbi Sholom Schwadron of Jerusalem. Reb Sholom was a famous *maggid,* a *talmid chacham* who gives exciting speeches filled with stories, and teaches people important lessons about Torah and how to be a better Jew.

Rabbi Krohn said to Rafi, "I have heard about Rabbi Schwadron. He sounds like a very interesting person. I would love to meet him. And if he ever comes to America, I would love to have him as a guest in my home."

"As it happens," said Rafi, "Reb Sholom is coming to America on Tuesday. He probably has a place to stay, but we can go to the airport to meet him."

Rabbi Krohn was very excited. He hoped he could have Reb Sholom as his guest. Right after Shabbos Rabbi Krohn went up to the third floor of his house and set up a room with a bed, a desk, a chair, a telephone, and a bookcase. The family waited excitedly for Tuesday.

Finally, it was Tuesday. Rabbi Krohn, his sons, and Rafi went to the airport.

When the plane landed and the people got off, it was almost sunset. Right away, Reb Sholom took out a compass to see which way was east. Then he opened his *siddur* and began to *daven Minchah.* The Krohn family watched in amazement as Reb Sholom *davened* in the noisy airport.

Then Rafi introduced Reb Sholom to Rabbi Krohn. He told Reb Sholom that the Krohns would like him to be their guest. To Rabbi Krohn's delight, Reb Sholom agreed.

When they came home, Rabbi Krohn showed Reb Sholom his room. After Reb Sholom unpacked his things, he came downstairs. "Thank you for making me so comfortable in your home, even though you don't know me. I would like to pay you for letting me stay here."

"No, no," said Rabbi Krohn. "We are so happy to have you as our guest! I do not want to take money from you."

But Reb Sholom would not stay without paying, so Reb Avrohom agreed to take the money.

A few days later, another rabbi from Eretz Yisrael, Rabbi Yisroel Grossman, joined Reb Sholom in the Krohn home.

During the next few months, Rabbi Krohn and his sons would sit around the dining-room table night after night, listening to Reb Sholom and Reb Yisroel teach Torah and tell stories about *tzaddikim*. The Krohns listened closely to every word, and learned new things every day from these two great men.

After a few months, it was time for Reb Sholom to go back to Jerusalem. Before he left, Rabbi Krohn gave Reb Sholom a large envelope. "Here is all the money you paid me during the last few months," he explained. "I never wanted to take money from you. I let you pay only so that you would feel comfortable in our home. I knew that if I let you pay, you would feel free to use the telephone, ask for special food, or invite a guest of your own."

Reb Sholom could not thank Rabbi Krohn enough. They hugged each other and said good-bye.

❊ ❊ ❊

The Schwadron, Grossman, and Krohn families have remained close friends to this very day. Their children and grandchildren learn Torah lessons from each other and help one another in many ways. My father, Rabbi Paysach Krohn, a son of Reb Avrohom Zelig, wrote the famous book, *The Maggid Speaks*, together with Rabbi Sholom Schwadron. Since then my father has written other Maggid books from which many people throughout the world have learned Torah lessons. And all this began with one act of *chesed* — because Rabbi Avrohom Zelig Krohn opened his home and his heart to two rabbis. That act changed the lives of his family members forever.